Running from the Rainbow

Karen McCombie

With illustrations by
Jessica Secheret

Barrington Stoke

For shy girl Ann!

First published in 2012 in Great Britain by
Barrington Stoke Ltd
18 Walker Street, Edinburgh, EH3 7LP

www.barringtonstoke.co.uk

This edition first published 2015

Text © 2012 Karen McCombie
Illustrations © 2012 Jessica Secheret

The moral right of Karen McCombie and Jessica Secheret
to be identified as the author and illustrator of this work
has been asserted in accordance with the Copyright,
Designs and Patents Act, 1988

All rights reserved. No part of this publication may be
reproduced in whole or in any part in any form without
the written permission of the publisher

A CIP catalogue record for this book is available
from the British Library upon request

ISBN: 978-1-78112-456-7

Printed in China by Leo

CONTENTS

Chapter 1

Spot the lie

Here are some facts about me.

1. My name is Rosie Roberts.

2. I am 12 years old.

3. I have a dog called Fred.

4. I am very shy.

5. My mum and dad are crazy.

Now that you have seen my list, can you spot the lie?

Here, let me help …

I *am* 12.

I *do* have a dog called Fred.

I *am* very shy.

My mum and dad *are* crazy.

So number **1.** is the lie.

Well, my last name *is* Roberts, but my first name is NOT Rosie.

I just call myself that.

My crazy parents called me something *else* when I was born.

They tell the story like this …

I was born in a storm.

Thunder crashed as Dad rushed Mum to the hospital.

Rain splashed on the windows as Mum pushed me into the world.

Then, as she held her tiny baby in her arms, the storm stopped.

Dad looked out of the window and gasped.

Mum looked too.

A rainbow ...

An amazing rainbow filled the sky.

Mum and Dad gazed at the wonderful colours. Then they gazed at me.

"Hey! Let's call her Rainbow!" said Dad.

"Wow! It's *perfect*!" said Mum.

Maybe Rainbow was a perfect name for a tiny baby, but it's not perfect when you grow up to be a very shy girl.

A shy girl with a crazy name.

If I tell adults what I'm called, they frown.

And at school they make fun of me. The other kids sing '*Over the Rainbow*' all the time. Or they call me 'Rain Cloud'. And who wants to be named after something grey and dull?

It's been no fun, that's for sure.

And now my crazy parents have told me we're moving.

I have to start again at a new school.

I don't want to go, and I don't want to say goodbye to my best mates.

But maybe there is ONE not-so-bad thing about moving.

I can be a new person.

A girl called Rosie.

And my *real* name can stay secret for ever.

Shhhh … Don't tell!

Chapter 2

First day, worst day

I feel sick.

At the end of the road is a big, modern building.

The sign outside says 'Manor Hill School'.

I start there today.

Unless I pass out with panic first …

"It's exciting, isn't it, Rosie?"

That's my mum talking. She's walking with me to school.

My mum thinks everything is "exciting". She's the sort of person who says "Wow!" and "No kidding!" and "That's amazing!" all the time.

Dad's like that too. Bad things can happen, sad things can happen, and he'll still find stuff to be happy about.

Even our dog Fred is loud and bouncy. His favourite thing is to chase his tail, barking. That's fine for a puppy, but he's ten, which makes him one very old, very daft dog.

Me?

Well, I'm the sort of person who doesn't say much.

And worries a *lot*.

Here's what I'm worried about today ...

Walking through the school gates.

Getting lost between classes.

No one talking to me.

Thinking of something to say if anyone DOES talk to me ...

"It will be great, Rosie, trust me!" Mum says with a smile. "Think about all the new friends you'll make."

She puts an arm around me, but I shrug her away.

"Look," she says, "I know you didn't want to move, Rosie, but this new job was too good for me to turn down!"

I understand what Mum is saying. Because of her work, we had to move house, move city, move schools.

So *yes*, I understand, but that doesn't mean I have to be happy about it!

"Can I tell you something, Rosie?" Mum asks now. She leans in closer to me. "I'm feeling a bit shy today, same as you!"

I stare at her.

She's wearing her best dress – the blue one with white polka dots. Her hair is very short and dyed very blonde. Her lips are red – the same red as the frames of her glasses and her red ankle boots.

She does not look shy.

She looks brave and bright and confident.

I look shy.

I am dressed in my new school uniform of a white polo shirt and grey skirt. Mum bought me a new pink rucksack, but I'm using my old, tatty navy one. I don't want to stand out.

I have my hair in a loose ponytail, with my fringe hanging in front of my face.

Dad says it makes me look like I'm hiding.

He's right – I am.

"Well, we're nearly there!" Mum carries on cheerfully. "Let's get on with our first day!"

Yes. It's the first day for BOTH of us. I will be a student at Manor Hill, and Mum will be a teacher.

At least she's not going to be *my* teacher.

That would be way too weird.

"Mum?" I say all of a sudden.

She looks pleased that I'm talking at last.

"Yes, Rosie?"

"You ARE going to keep your promise, aren't you?" I ask her.

"Yes! Yes, of course!" She nods.

I relax a little.

Then she spoils it all.

"But I still don't see why you want to keep your pretty name a secret!" Mum says.

Arrrggghhhh!

Mum makes me so mad sometimes!!

I moved here for *her*.

Why can't she just do this one thing for me?

"I'm going in on my own," I tell her, as I cross the street and hurry towards the school gate.

I sound grumpy, but I don't care.

"Bye!" Mum calls after me. "Have a good day!"

"I won't," I mutter to myself.

Chapter 3

Two parts of the promise

Will Mum keep her promise?

Will she keep my real name a secret?

I think so.

I hope so.

But what about the *other* part of the promise?

It's this – I have asked her not to tell anyone that she's my mother.

Why not?

Well, because she will be the pretty, cool and amazing Miss Ellis, the new English teacher.

All the students – and the staff – will think she is great, because everyone always does.

But I know people will look at her, and then me, and think, 'Huh? How can someone like Miss Ellis be the mum of such a dull, boring, shy girl?'

The truth is, I love Mum and she loves me, but we don't match.

So it's just a lot easier (for me) if no one knows we're related.

I just want to be plain Rosie Roberts. Then no one gets disappointed.

"New, are you?" a woman asks.

It's lunch, and I'm in the dinner hall. The woman is a dinner lady, standing behind a counter of hot food.

"Uh-huh," I nod. I can feel my face flush red.

"So, what do you want?" she asks.

The line for lunch is long, and kids keep pushing in. I look for a menu but can't see one.

"What is there?" I ask the dinner lady.

My voice wobbles, but the dinner lady seems to understand. She jabs a finger at lots of metal trays full of food and says what they are – but she says it way too fast.

I feel very muddled.

I don't want to ask her to say it all again – she'll get fed up with me, and so will the boys in the line behind me.

"Um ..." I mutter. "Can I have that, please?"

I point at the tray nearest to me and the dinner lady dollops some kind of gloopy pasta on my plate.

A few seconds later, I find an empty chair at a long table, and I sit down.

Three older girls are at the far end of the table. They don't look at me, so I don't look at them.

Instead, I prod my gloopy lunch with my fork and think about my first day at my new school.

So far, it's been a blur of new faces and endless corridors where I got really, really lost.

Different teachers going "blah, blah, blah".

Kids in class staring and staring and staring.

And me keeping my head down, down, down ...

Now girls and boys pass by my table, but no one sits beside me.

Good – I wouldn't know what to say to them. My mind is spinning *and* blank at the same time.

I stare at my pasta and try to think of home ...

My old home, I mean.

I remember my best mates Ella and Taylor, and all the lazy days we spent hanging out in the park. Long chats, ice-cream and Fred the dog chasing stuff, like other dogs, or squirrels, or his own stupid tail.

'Do Ella and Taylor miss me?' I wonder.

I bet they don't.

I bet they were only friends with me because they felt sorry for me.

They'll have a better time without me tagging along ...

"Look – over at the teachers' area! Check out the new Head of English!" I hear a voice say. It belongs to one of the older girls sitting at the far end of the table.

Her friend says, "What – you mean the one with the amazing hair?"

I want to peek, but just hide behind my hair and listen to the babble of voices.

"Her name is Miss Ellis," the first girl says. "I'm in her class."

"Are you? What's she like, Nina?"

"She's cool!" says Nina. "She told us she lived in Manchester before. She's married and has a 12-year-old daughter."

I shiver. What if these girls found out that was *me*?

"Huh?" says one of Nina's mates. "If she's married, why is she *Miss* Ellis?"

"Well, lots of teachers don't bother changing their name after they get married, do they?" says another of the girls.

That's true. Thank goodness Mum was one of those teachers. If she used her married name, she'd be Mrs Roberts. And that's way too close to Rosie Roberts!

"I wonder what her husband is like?" says the one called Nina.

"Look at the way she dresses ... I think she must be married to someone as cool as her."

"Maybe he's a photographer!"

"Or an artist!"

"Or a DJ!"

Ha! I giggle to myself as the girls make their guesses.

My dad – a photographer?

An artist?

A DJ?

I don't *think* so!

Dad has one of the most un-cool jobs in the world.

And that's yet another family secret I don't want anyone at my new school to find out.

Chapter 4

So many secrets

I can see Dad on the other side of the street.

You can't miss him.

He's wearing a green beanie hat, green T-shirt, long shorts with loads of pockets and chunky lace-up boots.

From the back he looks like he –

🖌 works in a garden centre, or

🖌 is an overgrown skater boy.

But Dad doesn't have a clue about flowers, and he has never even been on a skateboard.

It's not until you see the front of his T-shirt that you get an idea what his job is.

He's turning now, and giving me a wave.

'*Dogs On The Go!*' his T-shirt says.

Yes, my dad is a *dog walker*.

While families are out at work or school, Dad picks up their pups and takes them out for some exercise.

Where we used to live, he'd be in the park every day, with a big bunch of dogs following him around.

Now we've moved here, Dad needs to find new customers with new pets to take to our new park.

And that's why I have to meet him now. To put leaflets in letterboxes.

"Woooof! Woooofff! WOOOOFFF!"

"Down, Fred!" I tell our daft dog.

He's tugging at the leaflets in my hand, like it's a game.

"No! I'm *not* playing!" I tell him, and hold the leaflets up so he can't bite them.

But it's hard to stay cross with a dog that looks so funny.

He has a pink bow on his head today. Mum likes to tie the fur off his face with different coloured ribbons.

Everyone thinks that's sweet.

Strangers smile at him all the time, and stop and pat him.

They try to say stuff to me, but I just get shy and they give up.

"How's it going, Rainbow?" Dad calls out from the other side of the street.

I stop dead and frown at him.

"Dad!" I snap. "I asked you not to call me that!"

Dad grins as he crosses over. He puts his arm around me, pulls me close and kisses me on the cheek.

I push him away.

"Dad, it's not a joke!" I tell him. "You've *got* to call me Rosie!"

"What happens if I don't, my pretty Rainbow?" he teases me.

"What happens is I dump all your leaflets in the nearest bin!" I warn him.

"Aw, don't do that, Rain – I mean, Rosie!"

As Dad corrects himself, he tries tucking my hair behind my ears.

I just shake it loose again.

I'm helping him deliver these leaflets, so he can get some work. And all he can do is tease me!

"So how was your first day at Manor Hill?" asks Dad.

"You asked me that when I came home from school," I remind him.

"Yes, but all you did was shrug!" He grins.

I shrug again. I don't want to think or speak about today. Or how much I miss home, and Ella and Taylor.

"Hey, did you know your smile is the wrong way round?" Dad says. He pushes my mouth up at the corners with two fingers.

"Dad!" I snap, stepping away from him.

Here's what's going on ...

He wants me to say it's been OK.

That I was worrying over nothing.

That I have a bunch of new mates.

That I did not feel at *all* shy today.

But I can't lie just to make him and Mum feel better, can I?

I stomp off.

I'm going to post this pile of leaflets as fast as I can.

Then I'm going to go home and shut myself in my room.

(Maybe there will be emails from Ella and Taylor? Huh, I bet there *won't* ...)

BANG!! A door slams, somewhere up ahead. And look ...

A girl is coming down her garden path.

"Bye, Amy!" says a woman at the window.

"Bye, Mum!" the girl calls out as she shuts the gate.

With a shock, I see that she is from my class at school!

She turns and walks towards me.

No!!

There's no *way* I want her to see me!

What if she spots the stupid *Dogs On The Go!* leaflets?

What if she sees Dad and his stupid T-shirt?

What if Dad calls out my real name?

Lucky for me, Amy is looking at her mobile. I flip my hood up, bend down and rub Fred's head. But Fred ducks away from my hand and starts chasing his tail. I stay where I am, and hear the girl giggle as she goes by. She's giggling at Fred.

Thanks to my hood, she does not see my face.

She doesn't know it's me.

Is it always going to be like this? Me hiding who I am?

"Are you OK?" I hear Dad ask from just behind me.

"Yes," I lie, as a tear plops onto the pavement next to Fred's fat, furry paw.

Chapter 5

Spot the star

It's as if Mum is a pop star.

How crazy is this?

It's only her second day at school (and mine), but already she is a celeb at Manor Hill. From where I'm sitting in the playground I can see girls crowding around her.

She's wearing a swirly pink dress with a thick silver belt. The dress has no sleeves – she must be chilly. (I can feel spots of rain, and the wind is blowing grey clouds across the sky.)

But Mum looks as sunshine-y as ever.

One girl is patting Mum's short blonde hair, which is spiked up today.

From where I'm sitting I can watch what's going on. The girl's asking her a ton of questions. Mum is smiling and chatting. The shiny clips in her hair sparkle.

My mum is just a super sparkly person all round.

Same as my dad is fun, fun, fun.

Me?

I'm the small, dark cloud in my family ...

"Hi!"

I jump with surprise at the sound of a voice.

I'm perched on a low wall next to the school kitchen – where I'd hoped no one would spot me.

"Um, hi ..." I say back, looking up at the older girl who has appeared in front of me. She has a floppy fringe a bit like mine and a badge that says 'Prefect'.

She smiles at me. "You're Rosie – the new girl in Year 8, aren't you?" she says.

"Mmm," I mumble.

I feel panic rise in my chest. I'm no good at this – at talking to people I've never met.

"I'm Nina. I'm in Year 11," says the girl.

"Mmm," I mumble again.

Then I wonder if she's one of the older girls who was at my table at lunch yesterday. One of *them* was called Nina!

"How do you like Manor Hill so far?" she asks.

Yes, it sounds like the same girl. And how do I like Manor Hill so far? The truth is, not much.

But I don't say that. I just shrug, which is what I *always* do when I'm stressed out.

"If you're sitting here, I think it means you haven't got to know anyone yet," says Nina.

I look away from her and shrug again.

My heart is thumping in my chest. I sort of miss what she says next, but see that she has gone away.

Good.

But Nina's back in just a few seconds – and she's not alone!

"Rosie … this is Amy and Kim," she says. "They're in your class."

This Nina girl wants to help, I can tell, but she has done the *worst* thing.

Now there are THREE people staring at me, waiting for me to talk.

And ONE of them is the girl I saw yesterday, when I was delivering Dad's leaflets.

What am I going to do?

What am I going to say?

"I'll let you guys get to know each other!" says Nina, with a wave bye-bye.

So now there are only TWO people staring at me.

But I don't feel much better.

Kim speaks first, and then Amy. They ask me where I live, where I came from, what my old school was like.

I say "Stanley Street", "Manchester" and "OK".

That's all. I worry that if I try to say more, I may stutter with shyness. What will they think of me then?

Not much!

CRASHHHHH!

Now we ALL jump at the thunder that's just crashed above our heads.

WHOOSH!

Rain pelts down in a rush.

It's as if we're all standing under a giant shower, and someone has turned the tap on!

I can't help grinning.

Same goes for Amy and Kim.

As the rain soaks us, we turn from schoolgirls into drowned rats.

Our grins turn to giggles.

The three of us stand there, whooping at our soaked clothes and the mad rain.

It feels good – a bit like when I hung out with Ella and Taylor back in Manchester.

I'm totally wet but almost happy.

"Girls! Inside! Now!"

Who said that?

A teacher, of course. A teacher who happens to be my mum.

"You'll catch a cold standing out here!" she carries on, steering us towards the nearest door into school.

As we all run inside, I cross my fingers and hope she will go off to the staff room without saying anything else.

No such luck.

"Don't forget to look out of the window, girls," she says to us all, smiling. "Maybe you'll see a rainbow!"

Mum gives me a wink, then turns and goes.

Why did she have to say that? She thinks she's being funny, but there's nothing funny about saying my real name. Not even in a secret sort of way!

"Hey, why did Miss Ellis wink at you, Rosie?" asks Amy.

I shrug.

The feeling of happiness has gone.

I am back to being shy, stressed Rosie –
with a heart full of secrets.

Chapter 6

A secret slips out

It's Wednesday.

The sun is shining, the birds are tweeting and I feel a bit better.

As I stroll to school I think about what Mum said to me at breakfast.

"I understand why you're cross, Rosie," she'd told me. "And I promise I won't do anything like that again."

Back at home yesterday, she'd tried to make a joke of the 'rainbow' comment she'd made in front of Amy and Kim.

That had just made me even *more* angry with her, and I didn't talk to her all the way up to bedtime.

But this morning she'd looked so sad and sorry, like she finally understood how much she'd upset me.

So I think today I can relax a little.

And maybe I can try to talk a bit more to Amy and Kim ...

"Hey, Rosie!"

I turn around and see Amy. How funny is that – just when I was thinking about her?

"Um, hi!" I say shyly.

Amy catches up and we walk together towards the school gates.

"I took this today!" she says, holding up an umbrella. "Just in case the weather turns crazy again!"

We both smile at the memory of the sudden storm yesterday.

"It's hard starting at a new school, isn't it?" Amy says next.

"Sort of," I say.

"Do you miss your friends?" she asks.

"Mmm," I mutter, thinking of Ella and Taylor.

Ella sent me a text yesterday.

It said, '*How r u? When u going 2 email us all yr news? Luv Ella & Taylor.*'

I haven't got back to her. She and Taylor don't want to hear me moan about everything. They'd think I was moody and boring.

"My family moved house at the start of Year 6 …" Amy chats away. "And I hated my new –"

"ROSIE! ROSIE!!" shouts a man's voice behind us.

"WOOF, WOOF, *WOOFF*!!" a dog barks.

Amy and I spin around – and there are Dad and Fred, running down the road.

Dad is wearing his 'Dogs On The Go!' T-shirt, and has a roll of doggy poop bags in his hand. (Nice.)

Fred has a big purple spotty ribbon in his hair today, and a dribble of drool hanging from his chin. (Double nice.)

"You forgot your P.E. kit!" Dad says. He's panting from his run.

"Um, thanks," I say, and take the bag he's holding out.

There is silence for a second. I think Dad expects me to tell him who my new friend is. But I say nothing.

Then Fred jumps up on Amy, to say hello.

"Hey!" She giggles. "I think I saw this dog on my street the other day!"

"Ah, yes!" says Dad. "That's when me and Rosie were out delivering leaflets!"

I don't like him telling her that, but at least he's calling me the right name. Dad pulls one of the leaflets out of his back pocket and hands it to Amy. She glances at it – and then glances at me. Has she realised that *I* was the girl on her street, bent down and hiding under my hood?

"Wow! Got to go!" says Dad, looking at his watch. "Got to pick up some new dogs for their first walk!"

As he and Fred scamper away, I shoot a look at Amy.

What does she think of me?

"So your Dad walks *dogs*? That's his *job*?" she checks with me.

She's shocked, I'm sure of it.

"Yes. It's such a rubbish job ..."

"No, it's not – it's cool!" she says.

She doesn't mean that. She's just saying it to be kind.

"Please, Amy," I say, "please don't tell anyone!"

"But –"

"Please say you won't!" I beg her.

"OK, I promise," Amy says with a nod.

I've only just met this girl. Can I trust her with one of my secrets?

Maybe.

Maybe not.

I stuff my hands deep in my pockets as we walk on.

Amy can't see that I have my fingers crossed ...

Chapter 7

One secret out, two to go

The first noise on a Friday morning at school is this –

SCREEEEEEET!!

That's the sound of hundreds of chairs scraping across the main hall floor.

It's Assembly, and all the classes and year groups are trying to sit down and get settled.

"Shhhhh!" say lots of teachers, as we all shuffle and whisper.

I'm with Amy and Kim.

I still find it hard to say stuff to them, but they are taking care of me. The last two days, they have led me to classes, shown me the nicer toilets on the first floor, and chatted at break, while I've listened.

Maybe Amy is being nice because she feels sorry for me having a dad with such a useless job. (But I don't think she's told anyone.)

Or maybe she and Kim are only being nice because they promised Nina the Prefect that they'd look after me.

And look – there's Nina now, stepping onto the stage along with the other Prefects. As she sits down, she looks out into the crowd and spots me.

I feel myself blush as she waves her hand at me, and I wave back, blushing some more.

"Here comes Mrs Dennis!" Amy whispers, as a woman in a black polo-neck jumper and skirt comes onto the stage too.

Mrs Dennis is the Head Teacher of Manor Hill. This is the first time I've seen her. But I've heard about her before, as she's the one who gave Mum her job.

Which makes *her* the reason we had to move here.

At first, I'm thinking about that so much that I don't really listen to what Mrs Dennis is saying.

Then she says something I DO hear, loud and clear!

"And this term, we're pleased to have Miss Ellis join the English Department!" she says, and waves her hand to one side of the hall.

I sink into my seat as Mum stands up and waves hello at everyone.

She's wearing her green glasses today to match the green jewel clips in her blonde hair. Her dress is the colour of butter, with a tiny daisy pattern on it.

There are gasps all round the hall.

"She looks so sweet!" Amy murmurs.

"She makes all the other teachers look so boring!" Kim whispers.

"Can we all welcome Miss Ellis, please?" says Mrs Dennis. She claps her hands and nods at us all to join in.

When the clapping ends, Mum sits back down.

I hope that Mrs Dennis is going to move on to something else ...

"And it's not just Miss Ellis who came to Manor Hill this week!" Mrs Dennis booms in her loud voice.

'She's not talking about ME, is she?' I worry to myself, and try to slither further down in my seat.

"Her daughter has started in Year 8! So I'd like everyone to welcome her too!"

Amy and Kim turn to me with wide eyes. So do a lot of others in my class.

They have all just found out another of my secrets.

"Miss Ellis is your *mum*?" gasps Amy.

I don't say anything – Mrs Dennis has started saying something else.

"Where are you?" she asks, peering over to where all us Year 8s are sitting.

I slither further down.

"Can Rainbow Roberts stand up, please?"

NO!!!

She didn't even call me *Rosie*!

Did Mum tell her my *real* name?

Maybe she did, or maybe it's on my records. The office might have it on file.

"Rainbow?" Mrs Dennis repeats.

"*Rainbow?*" whispers Amy, with a frown.

That's it.

I stand up suddenly with a loud *SCREEEEET* of my chair.

And run, run, *run* as fast as I can.

I'm not just running out of the hall, I'm running away from my stupid parents and my stupid name ...

Chapter 8

Hiding from the hurt

"Rosie?" comes a voice from the other side of the door.

I'm in the first floor girls' toilets, in the last stall along, with the lock bolted shut.

I don't *ever* want to come out.

My head and my heart pound with the shame of what just happened.

"Rosie is *not* my name," I say to the person on the other side of the door. "Everyone in school gets that now, I'm sure ..."

In fact, Rosie was the name of a poodle that Dad used to walk. It went crazy when it saw me and always tried to lick my face.

(How sad is it that I named myself after a dog?)

"So do you want me to call you Rainbow, then?" says the voice.

It's Nina, the Prefect, I can tell.

She must have followed me out of the school hall.

Maybe she tried the downstairs toilets first, then worked out I must be here.

Maybe Amy and Kim told her this is where I'd be ...

"No!" I shout. "I HATE my name!"

I pull some loo roll off and dab at my eyes and my runny nose.

"But Rainbow is an amazing name!" says Nina.

She is standing so close to the door I can see her feet in the gap at the bottom.

"Amazing?" I say with a sniff. "You think so? Well, *you* try having a name like that! See how *you'd* like having everyone tease you about it!"

"They must have been very stupid at your last school," Nina says in a soft voice.

Her kind words make me cry again.

Kids at my last school *were* stupid. They saw how it upset me but they still did it. Even when Ella and Taylor told them to shut up.

"But I promise you, no one at THIS school is like that," Nina says. "Mrs Dennis always says that everyone is different and we must respect each other!"

I listen but say nothing, staring down at Nina's black pumps under the door.

"Here at Manor Hill, people will think your name is really interesting!" she says.

"No, they won't," I mutter, sure that can't be true.

"Yes it is!" Nina insists. "And Amy and Kim have told me they think YOU'RE really interesting!"

Me? Interesting? No way!

"But I find it hard to chat like they do. They'll soon get bored of me," I say, and I lean my hot head against the cool door.

"Look, when I started at this school, I was shy too," says Nina. "And here's a trick Mrs Dennis told me to try …"

As Nina talks, I find myself unbolting the door and opening it a crack.

"… if you don't know what to say to people, then don't panic," she says. "Just ask them stuff. Every time they answer, ask them *another* question! Everyone LOVES to talk about themselves!"

Wow …

That was such a good idea.

Such an easy thing to do.

Why didn't I think of that before?

"Here," says Nina, pulling me out of the stall. "Some people want to see how you are ..."

The door to the corridor is open, and Mum, Amy and Kim are standing there.

Mum rushes over to hug me, and I let her.

Amy and Kim stay where they are, staring at me.

"Are you OK, Rosie?" asks Amy, with a big, hopeful smile.

"I'm not Rosie," I say, smiling shyly back. "But I am OK."

And this time, I'm *not* lying.

Chapter 9

Another new start

All the dogs in the park are normal.

They are running, barking and catching balls.

But not *my* dog.

Fred has a baby blue ribbon holding the fur off his face.

He also has a daisy chain around his neck, made by Amy.

And he is chasing his tail. (Of course!)

"Your dog is nuts!" says Kim.

She grins and takes a snap of him on her mobile.

"Yep, he is!" I say, looking up from my phone.

I'm just getting back to a text from Taylor. She and Ella have been texting me like crazy every day.

That's after the long email I sent to them both. I told them how much I missed them, and how hard it had been to start at Manor Hill, and how my secrets had got out.

Nina was the one who told me to do that.

How come?

Well, Mrs Dennis the Head Teacher has let her be my 'buddy' – we hang out and chat at lunch most days.

Nina has helped me a lot.

Here's how ...

- She told me that my old friends would be missing me.

- She said I was being silly, thinking Ella and Taylor were glad I was gone.

- She got me thinking about how I come across to people. If I'm silent, they will see me as snobby, not shy.

Thanks to Nina, I'm still a bit shy, but I always smile now. And I'm better at chatting, because if I get stuck, I remember to ask people lots of questions.

The thing is, I won't ever be as sparkly and brave as my mum.

Or as funny and easy-going as my dad.

But I am me, and I am happy.

"Hey, Rain!" says Amy, taking her purse out of her bag. "Fancy an ice-cream?"

"Yes please," I say, with a smile.

I LOVE the new name that Amy and Kim and everyone calls me.

I'm not sweet Rosie.

I'm not bright and colourful Rainbow.

I'm Rain.

Not fancy. Just plain.

Pleased to meet you!

Our books are tested
for children and young people by
children and young people.

Thanks to everyone who consulted on
a manuscript for their time and effort in
helping us to make our books better
for our readers.